THE PLUMBER'S OBSESSION

WORKING CLASS DADDIES

EMMA BRAY

CHAPTER
ONE

Kyle

I TOSS my wrench in my toolbox and wipe my brow. I might not have the most glamorous job in the world, but it pays the bills.

Can't say I always said I dreamed of being a plumber when I grew up, but as a kid from the streets, I'm lucky I was able to make anything of my life. It would have been too easy for me to fall into the drug trap, but I got lucky when my foster parents adopted me.

Yeah, I know most foster kids don't get the luck I do, but I'm grateful every day for Cindy and Bob. They were kind old souls. They're gone now, but Bob was a good old guy. They always made sure I was fed and respected my feelings. They never pushed themselves on me, and Bob made sure he gave me some skills to survive in this world.

Hell, he even went a step further by leaving me his business when he died. My name might not be Bob, but I can't find it in me to change the name of my foster dad's business, so I still operate as Bob's Plumbing.

"You want another cookie, dear?"

I smile at Mrs. Molly. The widow has me over all the time doing all kinds of odd jobs for her in addition to handling her plumbing issues. I don't know why I can't get her to understand that she would save so much more money if she'd let me just redo her system instead of constantly coming over here and fixing it for her.

But then I finally realized that I think she wanted a reason to have to call me over to do some work for her. The poor old lady is lonely, and I know how that feels, don't I?

I've been lonely my entire life.

But she hasn't. She had her husband of fifty years, and when he died on her, she was left all alone.

So that's why I no longer try to talk her into upgrading anything. I just make sure I'm always a phone call away when her system shits out on her and she needs it fixed.

And I let her partially pay me in cookies.

It makes her happy, and I have to admit the woman makes a mean cookie.

I pat my abs. "They're good, Mrs. Molly, but you've already fed me a half dozen already."

She grins her snaggle-toothed grin. "A hardworking young fellow like you works up an appetite, though. Don't tell me you're watching your figure," she snorts.

I grin back at her. No, I have no need to watch my figure. I unashamedly eat like a horse, but I work out all the time when I'm not at work for lack of anything else to do, so I'm shredded.

That's why I sigh and accept yet another cookie from my most consistent client.

She chuckles and watches me like a proud grandmother as I scarf down the sugary morsel.

As I finish off my last cookie, Mrs. Molly stands up from her armchair, her eyes cutting over to me in supplication. "I have a favor to ask of you, dear."

I raise an eyebrow, intrigued. "Sure, thing, Mrs. Molly. You know I'll always do what I can for you. What kind of favor?"

She shuffles over to her mantelpiece and picks up a small photo frame.

I cock my head to the side as she ambles back over to me and hands me the frame. I look down.

And my entire fucking world comes screeching to a halt.

Inside is a photograph of a beautiful young woman smiling at the camera.

Fuck, she's young with perfect skin and bright blue eyes that shine like the morning sun. Her hair is golden and glinting in the sunlight. She's like a fucking ray of sunshine herself.

And I'm shocked when I feel my cock stir in my pants in response to just looking at her face.

"This is my granddaughter, Mandy. She just turned nineteen. She sent me this most recent photo this week. She lives across the country in California. I haven't seen her in years. I was wondering...could you fix my phone so I can Skype or Facetime or whatever you youngsters call it nowadays with her?"

"Mandy," I repeat, feeling the weight of her name on my tongue. It's a soft name, a name that sounds like it belongs to someone gentle and kind-hearted.

My mind is whirling as I try to come up with a response. I barely even know this woman, and yet looking at her photograph, I feel like I'm staring at someone I've known my entire life.

I can't believe my reaction to just a picture of her. I feel like a horny teenager who's never seen a pretty girl before. But I can't help the way my body is responding to her. I have to meet her, have to see her in person, have to find out what she smells like, what her voice sounds like, and if she tastes as sweet as the cookies her grandmother makes.

I move as if in a daze as I show Mrs. Molly how to use the Facetime feature on her iPhone. I'm hoping she'll call her granddaughter now so I can at least hear her voice, but no such luck.

Fuck.

But, fortunately, Mrs. Molly wasn't kidding when she said she knew next to nothing about cell phones and technology. That's why she never realized what I was doing when I forwarded a picture of Mandy and all her contact information to my own phone.

Call me a bastard, but I don't care.

I don't know what this is, but I *have* to find out more about this girl.

As I walk back to my truck, I can't shake the feeling that something is different. It's like a switch has been flipped inside of me, and I can't ignore the way my heart is pounding in my chest.

I've never been one for love at first sight or any of that mushy stuff, but looking at Mandy's photo, I feel like I'm seeing every-thing with a new set of eyes.

When I get home, I look up everything I can find out about her online. I stalk her social media profiles and stroke my cock to every picture of her face I can find.

And when I finally stumble across one of her in a little pink bikini standing on the beach with the sun setting behind her, I nut all over myself.

Jesus, I'm a sick puppy.

But I don't give a fuck because there's one

thing I now know for certain, and it's that Mandy is *mine*.

I don't know how I'm going to make this happen, but it *has* to happen.

Don't worry, Mandy, baby. Daddy's coming for you.

CHAPTER
TWO

Mandy

"DAMMIT!" I scream as I turn on my facet and water starts spraying everywhere.

Seriously, what the fuck?

Maybe I should have taken my grandmother up on her offer to go across country and live with her when my parents died.

But this is my home. This is the home where I grew up. This is where I have all my memories of Mom and Dad.

Tears fill my eyes.

I'm just not ready to let go of it yet. I know

it's just a house and that it's the memories I'll always treasure, but still.

I just can't do it yet.

Not yet.

The car accident was a year ago, but the cut is still too fresh.

I quickly turn the facet off. I'm going to have to do something about this, though, and while I don't really need to be spending unnecessary money, *this* is necessary.

I have to have the water working right.

I type on my cell phone with my thumbs looking for a plumber near me.

I don't even pay attention to the results. I simply click on the first name that pops up. One plumber is just like the next, right?

"Bob's Plumbing," a deeply masculine voice answers on the first ring, and I pause.

I don't know what I expected a plumber to sound like, but it's not the gruff voice on the end of the line. His voice is like iced whiskey being poured down my parched throat.

I swallow, suddenly nervous, though I don't understand why.

"Hi," I start, but my voice is shaking. "Um, I need my water fixed."

There's silence on the other end of the line. "Hello?" I wonder if we've been disconnected.

"Yes," his gruff voice has a hint of gravel in it this time. It's low and deep and something else I can't identify, though it's something that makes my toes curl.

"Can you help me with that?" I whisper, though I don't know why the fuck I'm whispering.

There's another pause before he answers, that voice sending tingles along my skin, "I can help you with anything you need help with, sweetheart."

I start chewing on my bottom lip as my cheeks flame. Are we still talking about my messed-up water? Because it sounds a lot like this guy is slipping all kinds of innuendo into every word he speaks, even though he's not saying anything out of the way.

"Okay," I answer back stupidly. "So, um, when can you come take a look at it?"

"Now." I blink at how immediate his answer is. "I'm on my way."

My brow furrows. "Don't you need my address?"

There's another pause and then the guy

chuckles. "Yes, of course. What's your address, sweetheart?"

I blush again at the way he calls me "sweetheart." Surely he can't mean it as an endearment the way it sounds. He doesn't even know me. He hasn't even seen me yet.

And I have no clue what he looks like either, but going off his voice alone, the guy sounds insanely hot.

I give him my address, and he rattles it off. "Yep, got it." I hear a door open and close. Then he says, "I'm on my way, alright?"

"Okay," I whisper. "I'll see you soon."

"I'll see you soon, sweetheart."

The call disconnects, and I stare down at my phone.

What the fuck just happened?

I don't know how long I stand there staring at my phone, but I have the sensation of heat enveloping me. It's starting at my toes and slowly making its way up my body.

I'm suddenly hot, burning up with an indescribable need.

I don't know what it is I need, but I know I need it, and I know I need it now.

I can feel the slick juice between my thighs. I'm wet and aching, and I have the sudden need to push my panties off and slide my fingers along my pussy.

And I've never felt like this before. I might be a virgin, but I've read plenty of books. I know what that feeling is supposed to be, but I'm totally confused as to why I'm having it over this faceless, nameless man I haven't even met yet.

Unless you count us meeting each other's voices over the phone?

I've never made myself orgasm, though I have tried to stroke myself like the heroines in my books do. I've just never been able to reach that pinnacle they always talk about.

I'm still chewing on my lip and pacing the floor, deep in thought about what all this could mean when there's a knock at my door.

I jump and stare at it, my heart thundering in my chest, my pussy still soaking wet for the stranger on the other side of it.

The plumber.

Shit.

CHAPTER
THREE

Kyle

I ALMOST GAVE myself away in my eagerness to rush over to Mandy's house without asking for her address.

I knew I'd be getting a call from her today because I'm the one who snuck into her house while she was asleep and fucked with her plumbing.

I also paid an obscene amount of money to make sure my business was the first one that would pop up in a search for plumbers in this area.

Is what I'm doing wrong? Yes. Do I give a flying fuck? No.

Mandy is *mine*.

From the moment I saw her photo at her grandmother's house, I've been obsessed with her. The very next morning I was on a plane out here to California to start over.

I've spent weeks just watching my little angel. She works at the zoo feeding animals, and I know her dream is to become a vet and care for them.

I watch over her every morning when she goes to work. Hell, I watch her while she's at work. And then I follow her home and sneak into her house at night and watch her sleep.

I'm probably the world's biggest creeper for doing that, but I can't help it.

What makes it worse is I stand there with a hard-on all night as I stare down at her. One night I finally gave in and stroked myself as I stared down at her sleeping form. I came harder and faster than I've ever come before, just barely catching it all in my hand to prevent making a mess all over her bed or floor.

I haven't been working, but I don't give a fuck. Making sure she's safe is more important. I'm not a big spender, so I've saved almost every dime I've ever made, which means I don't have to stress about not working now.

Not when keeping an eye on my Mandy is more important.

My cock is already growing, and my entire body is vibrating as I knock on her door.

I've been moving slow for the last few weeks, but that was only because I wanted to. I could have been here at her house weeks ago, but I wanted to make sure I knew every-thing about her first.

What she likes, who she spends time with, everything.

I know her life better than she does, and she doesn't even know I exist.

The door opens, and I feel like I just got hit in the chest with a baseball bat. I took photos of her, but nothing can compare to the real thing.

She's even more beautiful than her pictures.

I can't tear my eyes away from her as we stand there staring at each other. She's wearing cut-off shorts, and I'm willing to bet she's not wearing any panties under those short-as-sin things.

Fuck me.

"Kyle," I introduce myself by holding out my hand. It's not that I'm really that professional. I just want any excuse to touch her.

She blinks up at me. "I called Bob's Plumbing?" She says it as a question.

"Bob was the previous owner," I explain to her. "When he died, he left the business to me. I'm Kyle but figured I'd leave his name intact."

"Oh," she says softly, her wide eyes still staring up at me, those puffy pink lips slightly agape.

Motherfucker, those lips are killing me. Having them partially opened like that...all I can think about is how good it would feel to slide my cock between them.

I clear my throat and walk past her in an effort to discreetly adjust the huge tent my cock is pitching in my pants.

Don't need her seeing my raging hard-on and getting scared. That's all I need.

"Where's the problem?" I ask as if I don't know.

Mandy runs a hand through her beautiful

blonde hair, and I watch it ripple as it cascades over her shoulders.

Perfection. She's pure perfection.

I grip my hard-on hard through my pants, but it does no good. I can still feel the precum bubbling up out of it. It slides down the side of my swollen erection, making a sticky mess of my balls.

Fuck, never in my life have my nuts felt this full.

"This way," she says in that sweet voice of hers as she walks ahead of me and leads the way to the bathroom that's just off her bedroom.

I follow behind her, trying not to salivate like the dog I am at the way her hips sway and that perfect little ass of hers jiggles with every step she takes.

She's goddamn perfect.

My cock aches, and I have to tell myself it'll be worth the wait. You can't just go jumping on a girl like that after you just met.

You have to woo her a little. I've watched enough romance movies to know that.

"Water sprays everywhere when I turn the sink on," she tells me as she walks in front of me into the bathroom.

I force myself to concentrate on what she's saying and not on her ass—though it's a huge challenge.

I can feel my cock throbbing in my boxers, and I pray to fuck I don't have a wet spot on my pants from leaking so much precum.

"The hot water went out too," she tells me.

Just hot water? Wow. I thought for sure I'd fucked with the cold water in the sink too.

"I'll have to check everything out," I tell her, playing the part of the professional.

I really ought to be shot. If her father were still alive, I wouldn't blame him for putting a bullet straight through my head.

The things I want to do to this sweet girl are downright depraved.

I put my hand on my toolbox I brought with me and force myself to concentrate on the matter at hand.

Not how fucking horny I am or how much I'd like to shove my hard-on into her tight little pussy right here and now.

Not that I'd last long, but I could make it worthwhile for her.

I clear my throat, feeling the edginess of my desire for this woman. I'm like a goddamn raging bull around her.

"Okay," Mandy says. "Thank you."

I nod my head, a gesture that's automatic. I haven't been able to think of anything else besides what I'd like to do to her. It's fucking ridiculous.

"Hey, uh, Mandy," I say, turning around to face her.

"Yeah?" she asks, the sound of her sweet voice making my cock jerk in my pants.

I swallow as my gaze rakes over her. My hands ball into fists as I try with everything in me to restrain myself.

Christ, this girl lights up my world.

She fucking *owns* me, and she doesn't even realize it.

Hell, I don't even know what I was going to say to her. All I know is I wanted to see those beautiful blue eyes staring up at me again.

"Do you need something?" she whispers, taking a step toward me.

I take a step back, only because I don't want her to see how hard my cock is.

Her eyes are wide and warm, and she's fucking adorable.

Fuck, yes, sweetheart. I need something. I need you. Every piece of you.

I don't say that, though. "Do you mind if I get a glass of water?"

She smiles at me shyly as she nods. "Yeah, sure thing. Be right back."

I watch her leave the room and then quickly fix what I fucked with to make her have to call a plumber. By the time she returns, I flip on the facet and announce, "All fixed."

I feel like a piece of shit when she turns worshipful eyes on me and looks at me like I'm some kind of hero for fixing her water— the water that *I* fucked up in the first place just to get close to her.

She's so motherfucking sweet.

I want to wrap my arms around her and never let her go.

I fight the urge to do just that as she pushes the glass of water into my hands and smiles at me.

"Thank you," she says.

I close my eyes and suck in her perfume, deeply inhaling that soft, sexy little girl scent of hers.

Fuck, she smells good.

I want to breathe her in forever.

I feel her soft hand on my arm, and I open

my eyes.

"What do I owe you?" she asks.

"Nothing," I say quickly.

Her little brow furrows. "But you fixed the water."

"I'll bill you for it," I lie, holding her gaze. No way in hell I'll ever charge this babydoll for anything. I should be the one paying her for the privilege of standing in her presence.

Her eyes are searching mine, causing a weird fluttering in my gut.

The world seems to fade away around the two of us as we look at each other, standing so close.

The way she's looking me, I can almost imagine I'm the man she dreams about every night, and she's definitely the woman who holds my world in her hands.

At least my world...

She licks her lip, and my cock jumps in my pants.

I feel my heart start to pound, and I know my face has gone to shit.

I'm shaking like a motherfucker.

I'm so turned on I could shoot this goddamn load through my pants in a second.

I'll just have to control myself somehow.

"What?" she asks, her voice breathy and soft.

I don't answer her.

I *can't*.

I want her. I want her more than anything.

But I don't want to scare her away.

My chest is heaving up and down. I feel my nostrils flare. I probably look like a predator that's caught the scent of its pray, but damn it, she's driving me insane, and she's not even doing anything.

"Are you okay?" she asks me with a little tilt of her head.

I swallow.

She takes a concerned step toward me, and that step might as well be a match to kerosene.

I explode.

I feel precum racing up my shaft, and then it shoots out of my tip.

And I can't control myself any longer.

I grab Mandy and pull her flush against me. I grind my aching erection against her, humping her through our clothes like a depraved beast.

She gasps, and fuck if that surprised sound doesn't turn me on even more.

I can't think. All I can do is *feel*. Feel the way my cock tingles as I grind it against her little virgin mound.

I grab the back of her neck with one hand and angle her head up so I can finally kiss those puffy pink lips.

And my god, the moment I taste her...she's like the sweetest nectar. I could sip from her lips for the rest of my life.

My other hand goes down to her juicy little ass, grabbing hold of her and making sure that she's close enough to feel every fucking rock-hard inch of me.

Fuck, I can tell she's turned on. I can smell her sweet little pussy from here.

And that makes my head spin. The thought that my sweet Mandy wants me too is almost enough to make me pass out.

Fuck, I want to taste her pussy.

I want to plunge my tongue between those soft pink lips and slather my face in her sweet honey.

My cock throbs, and my balls tighten. I can feel my release on the brink. I'm about to come, but I'm not ready to let go just yet.

Not until my dick is buried deep inside her.

She moans again, and I reach down and slide a hand inside her shorts.

"Fuck, sweetheart, do you know how bad I want you?"

She gasps before she stammers, "But we don't even know each other."

Not true. I know everything about you, beautiful. "I know all I need to know," I tell her as I drop kisses along the smooth column of her neck and move my fingers to rub her wet slit.

She's so fucking wet, she soaks my digits.

"Look at you, baby," I praise her. "So wet for Daddy."

Her shocked gasp only makes me even harder.

"W-what?" she asks.

"That's right," I pull her tighter against me. Fuck waiting around. I'm laying my cards on the table right now. "You heard right, sweet thing. This little pussy needs a daddy to take care of it. You got one."

I rub her clit and feel moisture gush from her fuck hole. "Ohh," she moans as her head falls back.

Holy shit, I want her. I want to shove my cock into that sweet little pussy and fill her to the brim with my cum.

I want her to have my baby.

I want her to be *mine*.

"I want you," I growl. "I want you so fucking bad, sweetheart. Do you trust me to be your daddy and take care of you?"

It's a loaded question, and maybe I'm tricking her, but I don't give a fuck. There's no level I won't stoop to to get her to be mine.

Maybe she thinks I'm just talking about this one time, but I'm not. When Mandy says yes, she's agreeing to be mine forever whether she realizes it or not.

She licks her lips, her soft blue eyes hooded with lust before she finally nods her head, "Yes, Daddy."

Motherfucker. Hearing Mandy call me her daddy sends more precum racing up to my tip.

I waste no time. I grab my cock and press her against the wall, yanking down those fucking cut-off shorts that have been driving me crazy from the moment I laid eyes on her today.

She moans loudly as I slide my cock through her juicy little slit.

She's so fucking wet for me that my cock slides right in.

I watch her face light up in surprise as I tear through the barrier of her virginity.

"Fuck, so tight, sweetheart," I rasp as I hold her close to me, victory swelling my chest at being the first one to ever have her this way.

I'll be the *only* one.

She's mine.

Mine, mine, *mine*.

I've got my hands wrapped around her, pulling her down on me as I pump into her, hitting her at every angle, making sure every inch of me is buried in her pussy. With every thrust, I can feel her growing wetter.

The way her tight young pussy grips my cock short circuits my brain. I can't stop the truth from tumbling from my lips.

"You're so motherfucking perfect, Mandy. Everything about you. You get your daddy so hard. I'm motherfucking obsessed with you. Do you know that? Never going to let you go, sweetheart. You're mine. Do you hear me?"

Mandy is staring up at me with her mouth open in shock, but I know she likes what I'm saying because I can feel her pussy fluttering around me at my words.

"You like that, baby?" I cock an eyebrow at her.

She moans again, and I kiss the side of her neck, sucking hard on her sweet flesh.

I need to mark her as mine. I want to leave my marks all over her so she and everyone else will know she's *mine*.

"I'm going to make you my wife, sweetheart," I rasp into her ear, my cock twitching at the thought. "You're going to have my baby."

I pound into her, every word out of my mouth a promise to her.

She cries out as I fuck her harder. I'm trembling with my own release as I hold my throbbing cock deeper in her, threatening to come at any second.

Mandy feels me holding back and cries out, "Come in me, Daddy! I want to feel it!"

Shit. Those words are my undoing. I explode inside her, filling her with my cum and holding her flush against me.

I'm trembling as I realize what just happened.

I just made her mine forever.

I pull her against me, and she buries her face in my chest.

I simply stroke her hair for long moments, savoring the feeling of her still held in my arms until I finally tip her chin up so she's looking at me.

"Tell me what you're thinking," I whisper softly to her.

She bows her head again and bites her lip, those big blue eyes of hers staring down between us like she can't bear to look at me right now.

But I tip her chin back up to me.

She's so fucking beautiful. I could lose myself in her eyes.

And I do. I've lost myself in her.

"Mandy," I prompt her. "Talk to me, sweetheart. Tell Daddy what you're thinking."

I see her eyes hood again when I call myself her daddy, and my cock jumps in response. Fuck, my girl loves me being her daddy, and it's a good thing because I'm never going to stop.

"Is this crazy?" she asks me. "We just met this morning. This doesn't make any sense."

I drop a kiss to her lips to shush her. "Get out of your head, baby. Don't overanalyze it. Does it feel right?"

Her eyes search mine before she nods slowly.

"Then, why does it matter if we just met? Who says we have to have known each other for a certain amount of time? When you know, you know, right? And, Mandy," I tighten my arms around her. "I fucking know, okay? I know you're mine now, sweetheart, and I'm never going to let you go. I'm going to take care of you forever. You believe me, honey?"

Mandy smiles at me shyly before she bobs her head and wraps her arms around my neck.

"Good girl," I praise her before I crash my lips back down to hers.

I'm determined that before this day is through Mandy will be as wrapped up in me as I am in her.

Mandy

THE DAYS since I met Kyle have been a blur. We've been inseparable. We spent all weekend in tangled limbs of passion in bed, and during the week, he drops me off and work and picks me up and then we have dinner together and make love all night.

I've never felt as close to someone as I do him, and it still boggles my mind that I never would have met him had it not been for my fucked plumbing.

What are the odds I would find my soulmate in the yellow pages? Well, the first page of search results on Google, but it's the same difference.

It's all so surreal, but I'm completely wrapped up in him. He makes me feel something I've never felt before.

Cared for, adored, safe.

And the thing about him calling himself my daddy isn't that I have daddy issues because my dad and mom died in a car accident. My father and I had a good relationship when he was alive.

No, this is something different. It's not like we're getting off on the idea of Kyle being my actual father. It's more like he's my protector, the one I know I can turn to with anything, the one who will take care of all of my problems, the one who will fulfill me sexually and otherwise.

And fuck does he fill me. My pussy starts throbbing just thinking about the possessive words Kyle growls in my ear as he comes hard inside me until it's flowing down my thighs.

It's not that I particularly want a baby yet, but hearing Kyle promise to breed me and seeing how crazy the thought drives him turns me on to no end.

He must work the same hours as me because every moment that I'm off work is spent with him.

He spoils me. He does everything for me he can and tries to keep me from lifting a finger like I'm a princess or something, and while I love it, I'm used to doing things on my own, so I try to help him out as much as he'll allow.

He lets me help in the kitchen, though most nights, he already has everything cooked when I get off work. He comes and picks me up and takes me home and then sits me on his lap and feeds me.

It's not that he's treating me like a baby either. No, it's more like it's an intimate thing, and strangely enough, it's highly sexual the way he feeds me each bite. By the end of every meal we eat that way, we barely make it out of the kitchen before he's slamming his cock inside me and roaring to the world that I'm his.

Sometimes we don't even make it out of the kitchen.

I squirm as I remember the way he threw me over the kitchen table and spread me wide before he ate me out and made me come all over his face.

"What are you thinking about, sweetheart?" Kyle's voice interrupts my thoughts, and I blush.

He grins at me wickedly as he lifts me onto the edge of the counter and spreads my legs, pushing my dress us as he does so. "Is my little girl thinking about her daddy's mouth on her wet little pussy?"

"Yes," I admit with a husky whisper.

"Hmmm," he moans directly in my ear. "You like the way Daddy flung you over this table and made you his dessert yesterday?"

"Kyle," I moan out his name as his fingers stroke me through the thin fabric of my panties.

"Daddy," he reprimands me. "You call me daddy when my hands, tongue, and cock are touching this pussy."

"Daddy," I sigh as he pushes a finger into me and continues to rub circles on my clit at the same time.

"You like that, don't you, sweetheart?" he teases me before biting my neck.

"Yes," I moan as I start to rock my hips against his hand.

"Oh, I know you do, baby," he growls as he rubs me faster. "I know you like when daddy licks your pretty little pussy. I know you like when daddy makes you come on his face. I know you like it when daddy fucks your tight little hole," he groans as he thrusts another finger into me.

"Oh, god," I moan as my eyes nearly roll back in my head.

I feel Kyle unbuckling his belt and dropping his pants as he continues to rub me to my orgasm.

"Daddy," I moan as I feel his cock press into me.

Kyle slams into me so hard I slam forward on the counter, and he grunts loudly as he grabs my hips and grinds into me.

"Oh, god, Daddy," I moan out as my pussy clenches around him.

"That's it, baby. Daddy's going to fill you up now," he growls out. "Daddy's going to fill his sweet little girl's pussy with his cum. You want it, sweetheart?"

"Yes, Daddy. Fill me up!"

And he does just that. I feel his cock twitch and pulse as he releases his cum inside me, and it takes my own orgasm right over the edge with his. I come so hard I gasp, struggling to catch my breath.

"That's it, sweetheart," he groans as he holds himself deep inside me. "That's it," he moans as he pumps his cum into me.

"Daddy," I moan as I feel his cock finally deflate.

"Now, I'm going to carry you into the bedroom," he tells me as he starts to pull out of me. "And I'm going to lay you on that bed and spend the rest of the night worshiping every single inch of you."

"Yes, please, Daddy," I nearly sob as he pulls his hands from me.

"How did you get your panties so wet, little girl?" he asks me as he pushes me off the counter and picks me up in his arms.

I blush as I look up at him. "I was thinking of you."

"Mmm, I love it when you think of me like that, sweetheart," he whispers against my lips before kissing me so deeply I think I might come from it alone.

After he fulfills his promise to worship every inch of me, I lay across the bed limp as a ragdoll while he gets up to go to the bathroom.

I smile lazily to myself and stretch like a contented kitten. I close my eyes to doze off, but a ringing catches my attention.

I roll over onto my side and freeze when I see the name flashing across Kyle's phone screen.

That's my grandmother's name.

My brow furrows as I pick up Kyle's phone and stare down at it in confusion. Why does he have my grandmother's name in his phone? How does he know her?

Kyle comes striding back into the room buck-naked, but I see him freeze when he sees me holding his phone in my hand.

My stomach drops at the guilty look on his face.

I hold the phone up and point at the screen. "How do you know my grandmother?"

Kyle never breaks eye contact with me as he moves slowly toward me as if I'm a frightened animal that's going to bolt at any moment.

"Sweetheart," he starts in a gentle voice that sends shivers down my spine. "You know I'd never hurt you, right?"

"Why do you have my grandmother's

number in your phone?" I ask him again through clenched teeth.

He stops in front of me and kneels down, taking my hand. "I know you're upset, sweetheart, but let me explain."

I just stare at him, waiting, my heart fluttering in my chest.

"How do you know her?" I try to ask him calmly when he doesn't volunteer an explanation.

"I knew her in Boston," he tells me softly, and I feel my breath catch in my throat at his words. "I was a plumber out there—where I'm from. That's how I found out about you—through her."

"What?" I whisper, shaking my head in confusion. "What are you talking about? We met when you came out here to do a plumbing job."

"Oh my god," I cover my mouth with my hand as the pieces start to click together.

"We're not soulmates," my voice breaks. "I knew it was too good to be true. How did it happen? You somehow found out about me and orchestrated this whole thing? Why?"

I scoot back on the bed to put some distance between us, but Kyle isn't having it.

He pounces on me and stills me with a hand on either side of my hips. His eyes blaze down into mine, and his voice is desperate as he confesses, "Yes, Mandy. Your grandmother wanted me to help her learn how to Facetime so she could talk to you. She showed me a picture of you, and I became motherfucking *obsessed* with you. Don't ask me why or how. All I know is one look at your picture, and I was a goner."

I swallow as his words crash over me. "So, you stalked me?" I ask hesitantly.

"Call it what you will," he shakes his head, "but I don't regret a minute of it because just look at us now, baby."

He grabs my face in the palms of his hands. "You know I'm meant to be your daddy, and you're my little girl."

Heat pools between my thighs at his words, but I shake my head.

"But, how did you know we would meet?" I'm so confused.

"I fucked with your plumbing," he confesses. "I did. I orchestrated it all, Mandy, but I didn't know how else to approach you. You make me insane. I had to do anything I could to get close to you. Please tell me you understand. Please tell me you forgive me. Please, Mandy."

I just stare up at him as my mind struggles to process everything he's just thrown at me.

"Please, Mandy, say something." His voice breaks, and I look up at him, startled to see tears in his eyes.

Kyle is such a guy's guy. He's a total alpha male with all those grown-man vibes, and it's humbling to see him crying.

Over *me*.

"I know it was wrong, Mandy. I know that, but I'm not sorry. I'm being honest, baby. All I want is you. You're all I've ever wanted even when I didn't know it. You're what I was looking for when I didn't even realize I was looking. I can't lose you, Mandy." His grip tightens on my hips as his eyes take on an almost crazed look. "I can't."

I'm quiet for a long moment as I consider everything he just confessed. I should be scared.

Should be.

But I'm not.

"Okay," I whisper as I take his face in my hands. What he did might not be right, but I don't really care.

I don't want to lose him either.

In fact, maybe I'm crazy too because I kind of *like* the thought that he's *that* obsessed with me.

"Okay?" his eyes search mine before he falls to his knees in front of me and starts planting reverent kisses all over my tummy.

"Fuck, Mandy. You're perfect. I don't deserve you, sweetheart."

I drop down to my knees in front of him. He shakes his head against mine before he kisses me fiercely on the mouth. "I'm going to spend the rest of my life being everything you need. I'm going to give you everything I can, Mandy. I promise you."

My heart swells at the look of utter devotion on his face, and I know that no one will ever love me the way this man does.

"I love you, Kyle," I choke out.

"I love you too, baby," he whispers as he crushes me against his naked chest. "I've loved you since the moment I first saw you in a picture. You've always been mine."

"And I always will be," I reassure him as I curl close to his chest, safe in his arms.

Where I belong.

EPILOGUE

Two Years Later

Kyle

MY COCK HARDENS as I watch Mandy walk out of the college classroom.

I wait for her every day and pick her up after her classes are done—just like I used to pick her up from work every day. Only now, she's not working. I'm putting my girl through college so she can achieve her dream of becoming a vet.

I know she can do it. She's the most brilliant woman I've ever known, and I couldn't be prouder of her.

She catches my eye and gives me an impish grin. She knows what that little schoolgirl skirt does to me. And the way she's got her white blouse tied up to bare her perfect stomach.

Fuuuck.

A growl rumbles up in the back of my throat at all the glances the males cast her way. I can't really blame them for their double-takes. Mandy is the most beautiful creature to ever walk this planet.

The only thing that calms me is the way my girl's eyes never leave mine.

She has eyes only for *me*. Her daddy.

As soon as she reaches the car, I grab her and pull her into my lap, starving for her kiss.

She kisses me back voraciously, her little tongue dancing with mine, driving me insane.

I reach down between us and hiss in a breath when I find she's not wearing any panties.

"You naughty little girl. Does your daddy know you snuck out of the house dressed like that?"

"He does now," Mandy moans as she

begins to grind her soaking wet pussy on my aching hardness, making a mess on my jeans.

"Mmmm, what are we going to do about this leak, baby? You're gushing fluid everywhere."

"Maybe my daddy can fix it?" Mandy moans as she wraps her arms around my neck and grinds harder on me.

I still her with a hand to her hip as I grind myself back up into her. "Oh, I think your daddy can plug that little hole up. He's got just the tool for the job."

"Fuck!" Mandy screams as she rocks her hips against mine frantically.

"Yes, that's it, baby. Come while you grind that soaking wet pussy all over your daddy's cock."

"Kyle!" Mandy screams as she falls apart in my arms.

"Fuck!" I can't take it anymore. Seeing Mandy tip over the edge while humping me is more than I can take. I unzip my pants and fist my cock, lining it up with her soaking wet hole.

One hard thrust and I'm inside her. My cock slides in easily because she's so slick.

After two years of doing this, we know

every way to make the other one's pleasure rock the other's world.

I fuck her like an animal, pulling Mandy up onto my lap so she's facing me as I drive into her.

Mandy cries out again as she rides me hard. The friction against my cock makes the pleasure almost painful. I feel my orgasm building, and I know that I'm not going to last much longer.

Mandy tightens the walls of her pussy around me, milking me. She knows what my body needs even before I do.

"Motherfucker!" I roar as my climax finally hits me. My seed rockets up my stalk and vomits violently into her pussy.

She's spasming around me as we come together, jerking and pulsing around each other.

I draw her lips to mine, making out with her as we ride out our orgasms together.

Fuck, it feels so damn good to be inside her. This is where I belong.

"I love you," Mandy pants as she rests her forehead against mine, both of us trying to catch our breath.

"I love you too, baby. I fucking love you so much," I tell her as I kiss her cheek.

She's my everything.

The love of my life.

And now, she's my wife.

I slide a hand down to her stomach where we're expecting our first child.

A man can't be any happier than I am right now.

I look at my new wife and know that this is the beginning of a whole new adventure that I want to experience with her.

Forever.

Want more Emma Bray? Go to www.authoremmabray.com to sign up for Emma's newsletter and get a free book!

Keep reading for a sample of The Trucker's Obsession!

Chapter 1

Blake

. . .

I pull into the truck stop and put my big rig into park. I sigh and wipe a heavy hand across my brow before I lean my forearms on my steering wheel and look out my windshield.

I can feel the silence of the truck stop, interrupted only by the rumble of my engine as it slowly fades away. The parking lot is empty but for the occasional car and truck, but nothing is moving. It's like no one is here, but I know there are plenty of other truckers here too. They're just probably all asleep in the backs of their rigs.

The sun is setting, casting long shadows across the highway and the parking lot. The dull hum of the buzzing fluorescent lights spills into the air, creating a strange sense of eeriness. The silence is so thick it feels like a blanket, enveloping me in its embrace. I can feel it, like a heavy weight pressing down on me.

There is something hauntingly beautiful about this moment, something that stirs a deep longing inside me. I don't know what it is or why it is so strong, but I can feel it in my bones. The stillness, the solitude, the absolute quiet. I find myself yearning to be part of it, to exist in this moment for just a little while longer.

I reach up and turn off the engine, plunging me into complete silence. The only sound I can hear now is my own breathing, and it's the only thing that I can focus on. I take a few deep breaths, and it feels like I am finally able to relax. I let my head rest on the headrest and close my eyes, taking in the peacefulness of the moment.

The dull hum of the fluorescent lights has become a melody in my ears, and I can feel the entire truck stop like an extension of my own body. I take it all in, from the way the asphalt shimmers in the fading light to the way the shadows seem to stretch out for miles.

I feel the loneliness.

It is a feeling I know all too well, the heavy burden that comes from feeling completely alone. The sun is almost gone now, and the sky is a soft, fading shade of blue.

I exhale another breath and reach for the handle of my truck.

And then I go completely still.

My heart starts beating in overdrive, and every muscle in my body tightens when I see her.

I don't have a clue who she is, but she's the prettiest little thing I've ever seen in all my thirty-two years.

She's an angel.

No, she's a *goddess.*

Her long, red hair flows down over a backpack to an impossibly tiny waist. It's wild and untamed, like a lion's mane. She can't be more than five-foot-four and thin, but she still has a nice handful of curves.

She's nothing short of glorious.

But what the fuck is she wearing?

My cock is a rod of steel as my eyes sweep over her from head to toe. Her white tank top doesn't completely cover her stomach, leaving the expanse of skin just below her belly button and between the hem of her shorts exposed.

And *fuuuck,* those shorts.

They shouldn't even be allowed to be called shorts. They barely cover her ass, and while I'm loving the view, I'm instantly, irrationally enraged and jealous at the thought of other men seeing her like this.

And I know that's insane when I don't even know her.

My insanity goes up a notch when I see several men's heads turn in her direction as she makes her way to the door of the truck stop.

A low growl bubbles up in my throat when I see them blatantly checking her out.

I panic when I see some of them starting to follow her.

Jesus, she's going to start a riot if she's not careful. I see the looks in their eyes. They're thinking the same thing I am, but the difference is I want to take care of her.

I want to be her protector.

And I make my decision here and now.

I fling open the door of the truck and cast threatening glances at every man following her.

She is *my* woman.

Alicia

I don't know what my plan is. All I know is that I had to get out of *there*.

My stepdad has always been a creep, and now that I'm eighteen, it's all I can do to keep him at bay.

I might be a virgin, but I know what the looks he gives me mean.

And when he started openly palming himself tonight while he looked at me, every alarm in my head started going off—especially when he started drinking.

I didn't know how much longer I could hold him off, so I jetted out of there.

I frown. It's a bit earlier than I wanted to leave. Well, *wanted* isn't the correct term. I've never wanted to be there with him, but, unfortunately, he's the asshole I was left with after my mom split on me.

Yeah, my mom ran off and left me with her new husband. Too bad she never knew who my dad was. I'd rather she had left me with my real father a long time ago instead of the asshat she married and then decided she didn't want to be with anymore.

Apparently, she decided she didn't want to be a mother anymore either.

But I'm not crying about it. It is what it is. She was never much of a mother to me anyway. I always felt like a tag-along, a hindrance to her.

Mom was always more concerned with partying and meeting guys than making sure her daughter was fed and taken care of.

So, I've been taking care of myself for a long time.

And while I never wanted to stay with Jeff, it was a roof over my head while I tried to scrimp and save what I could to get me a start in life. Plus, it was much better than being in the foster care system. I knew kids who were in it, and as long as I could stay away from Jeff as much as possible, I figured I could put up with his leers.

But he was fixing to start making advances. I could tell.

So, I had to leave sooner than was ideal, but I'm confident I'll be able to make it on my own.

I readjust the backpack on my back. I don't have much in it, just the little bit of cash I made washing cars and the few scraps of clothing I was able to grab before I left my stepdad's.

I don't need much, and besides, too much stuff and I wouldn't be able to carry it all.

My tummy gives a growl. I wish I'd had the foresight to grab a few granola bars at least.

As I step into the truck stop, I'm instantly assaulted by the aroma of food. My mouth starts watering as I glance longingly at the plates of burgers and waffles some of the truckers are eating.

A hot meal looks great, but I chew on my bottom lip as I consider how much cash I have. It would be smarter for me to buy something from the convenience store so I can stretch my money further.

I turn from the diner to head to the convenience store side of the truck stop and gasp when I collide into what feels like a brick wall.

But when big hands reach out to gently grasp my upper arms and steady me, I realize that what I ran into is not a wall but a *man*.

A really, really big man.

My head turns up, up, up to a guy who's got to be at least six-foot-five. He's more than a foot taller than me, and he's nothing but bulging muscle everywhere.

I'm not one of those girls who swoons over super ripped guys, but my face is suddenly flaming, and I feel all sorts of fumbling and stupid.

"Oh," I stammer. "I'm so sorry. I didn't see you there."

He doesn't say anything at first. Instead, his blue eyes just smolder down at me.

I can't help but stare. I've never seen eyes that color before, and he's got a strong, square jawline, with a firm bottom lip.

But what really blows me away is his hair. It's thick and dark and shaggy, and I wonder what it would feel like to have the strands fall across my bare, aching breasts.

The thought is embarrassingly inappropriate and for a second, I feel myself flush again, but this time there's a different sort of warmth in my belly.

His hands tighten on my arms, and his nostrils flare. I see the muscles in his arms flex, and his chest starts heaving up and down as he continues to stare at me.

"What's your name, dollface?"

I blink, caught off guard but hear myself answer him, "Alicia."

"Alicia." He repeats my name with a note

of wonder in his voice, and I press my legs together to ease the throbbing between my legs.

Why am I reacting to this man this way?

My body trembles, and he frowns when he feels it, his eyes skating down over me.

"You cold, honey?"

I melt a little more at the way he calls me 'honey.' And hell no, I'm not cold. I'm on fire, but I nod my head anyway.

"It's no wonder," he grumbles, his eyes heating as they flick over me disapprovingly again. "You're barely wearing anything."

"What?" I stammer as I look down at myself. I'm just wearing shorts and a tank top. "What's wrong with what I'm wearing?"

He barks out a strained chuckle as he leans so close to me his breath skims over my ear, making me shiver again. "Have you not noticed that every man in this truck stop is staring at you?"

My face flames as I turn and look around and finally notice what he's talking about. There *are* several pairs of eyes on me, and they all wear the same lecherous look my stepdad used to give me all the time.

I subconsciously press closer to whoever

this huge man is, my eyes widening when I feel something impossibly hard pressing against my ass.

I tilt my head up to look back at him, and he's staring down at me with a look in his eyes that makes my breath catch.

"You never told me your name," I whisper.

"Blake." His voice comes out husky and rough, like sandpaper.

"Blake," I repeat his name just like he did mine, and I feel that hardness jerk against my backside.

He doesn't even try to hide it. Instead, he growls and grips my hips. "You're enough to start a war, you know that little girl? Who let you out of the house like that?"

I don't know why, but his comments make me flush with pleasure. "No one," I say. "I'm eighteen. I can do what I want."

He pulls me closer to him, subtly grinding that huge part of himself against my ass. "Like hell you can," he growls in my ear where only I can hear. "Look around, honey. These men are hungry wolves, and you're the prey they're wanting to fight over. You need an alpha who's going to protect you."

I peek another glance up at him, my heart

racing at his words and his close proximity. This has got to be the craziest thing that's ever happened to me, but I'd be lying if I said I'm not digging every minute of it.

"You're an alpha?" I whisper as he runs his hand down my arm.

He doesn't answer. Instead, he laces his fingers through mine and pulls me along with him towards the truck stop restaurant. I want to question him, but the further we get into the restaurant, the more I'm distracted by how many people are staring at us.

I'm not just talking about the dinner crowd. There's an entire family at the table with their eyes glued to the way Blake leads me to our booth and slams himself in the seat across from me.

Blake ignores them completely, his eyes locked on me. "Stay here," he says.

He leaves me there, stunned and trembling with excitement, and strides to the counter.

I watch as he orders two coffees and two double cheeseburgers with fries.

He carries the food back over to the table and places it all in front of me.

My face flames as my tummy gives

another embarrassing growl, but Blake merely orders, "Eat."

I don't try to feign a lack of hunger. Instead, I eagerly obey and dig in like I haven't eaten in a week.

Actually, I haven't eaten much in a week—just cans of soup mostly. I can't really remember the last time I had a burger and fries.

Blake watches every bite I take as he inhales his own food. His eyes never leave me. I feel like I'm the center of attention, and it's not just because everyone is staring at me. It's Blake

He's gorgeous. I can't stop thinking about it. In fact, I don't even want to try to stop.

I don't know how someone can simply look at a person and make them feel so protected and safe. I might be stupid, but I can smell the testosterone and dominance coming off this guy in waves. He's just oozing power, and I want to bask in it.

And then my body reacts. I blush, the color rising all the way up to my roots. I'm almost sure I'm turning the same shade of pink as the hot pink shirt the chick with the red hair and the glasses at the table next to us is wearing.

I bow my head and stare down at my plate as I continue to eat as slowly as I can.

I'm not sure why, but I don't want this to end. I'm not even sure what this is, but I don't want it to end. I want to sit here with Blake and not have to worry about anything other than whether or not I'm going to finish eating this entire burger. I want to sit here with him and muse over the fact that he could probably bench press me.

I'm not sure how long I sit there with my head down, but I know it's too long by the time I look up.

Blake is staring at me with a concerned—almost angry-looking—furrow in his brow. "What are you running from, dollface?"

I consider trying to keep my business to myself and denying that I'm running from anything, but something about this man pulls the truth straight out of me.

"My stepdad."

Blake growls, his hands flexing where he's got his forearms laid on the table.

"Where you planning on going?" he asks me, his voice sounding taut.

"I don't know," I whisper.

His fingers flex again, and his jaw hardens as another growl rumbles up out of that big chest.

Why does that make me clench my legs together?

"Well, I do," he states.

"You do?" I ask, my voice breathless and my eyes wide.

"Yes," his gaze latches onto me as his eyes sweep over me possessively.

"You're coming with me."

www.ingramcontent.com/pod-product-compliance
Lightning Source LLC
Chambersburg PA
CBHW021351160726

47994CB00007B/2914